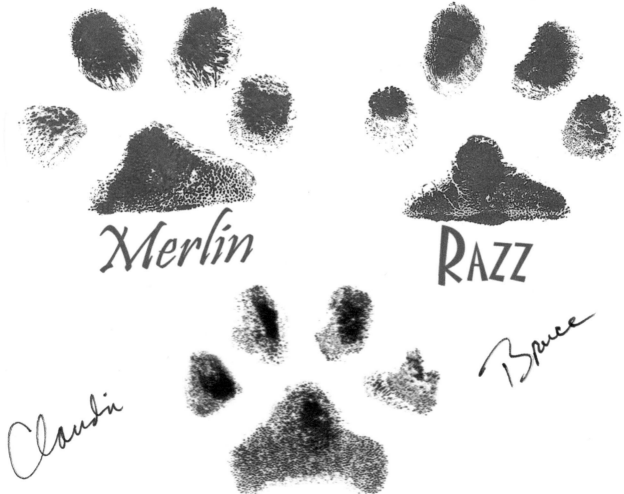

Happy Tails,

Merlin

Razz

Whimze

Claudia

Bruce

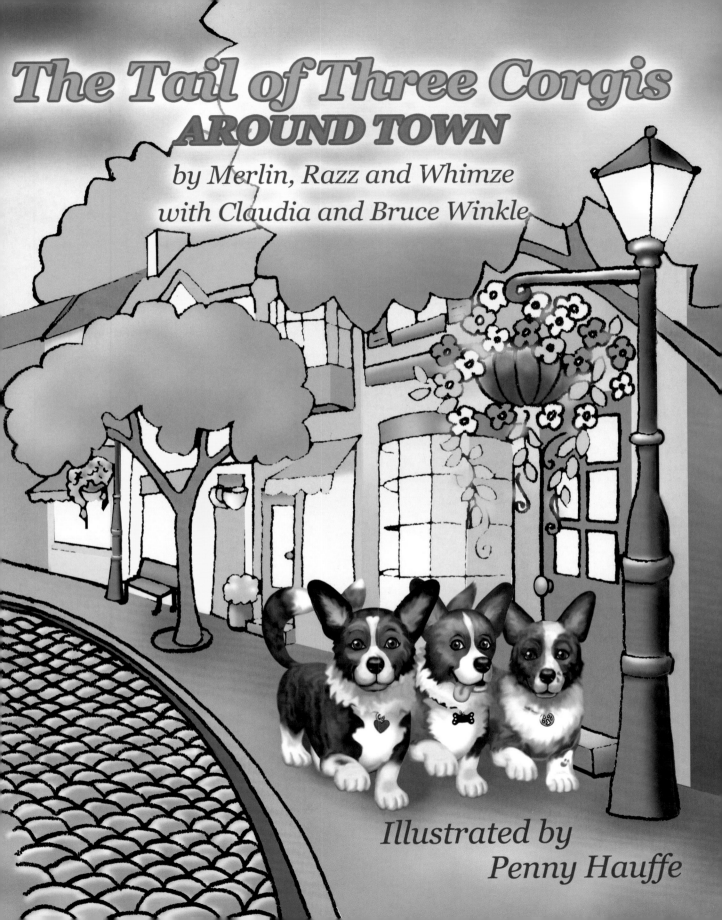

The Tail of Three Corgis
AROUND TOWN

by Merlin, Razz and Whimze
with Claudia and Bruce Winkle

Illustrated by
Penny Hauffe

In remembrance

of

Rupert.

Printed in USA
US $16.95

Published by: Merrazz-LLC
ISBN# 1-978-0-9846868-3-4

First Edition 2016

Hi!

We are Merlin, Razz and Whimze,

the Cardigan Welsh Corgis.

You know, the Corgis with the tail.

Tag along with us as we

travel around town.

One of our favorite things to do is

just walk in the park.

We go to the health food store for
gallons and gallons of goat milk.

This is the secret (ssshh!)
to our soft and silky coats.

Time for our annual check-up.
First we have to weigh in.

Oops!

We have put on a pound

or two

or three.

SCALE

The Doctor says,

"Time for the treadmill..."

We are celebrating our new book.

Please enjoy a **Corgi** shaped cookie or a cupcake!

We help dad pick up our delicious and nutritious dog food.

We all get a tune-up
at the chiropractor's.

It's like a three ring circus in our yard.

Come join our Corgi fan club

for our first Friday book signing.

about the Cardigan Corgi breed.

We play
hide
and
seek
while Mom shops for
delightful dahlias.

Oh my gosh!

The dahlias

are as big as

our dog bowls!

It's almost time for the party.
Let's wrap the present
we purchased for the pretty poodle.

we get to swim and splash!

Blessings to all God's creatures

big and

small.

Blessings to us all.

After our busy schedules

we take time to

z o n e   o u t

Thank You
to all our friends around town.

Angela 'A' Dogwalker
Angela Snook

MJ DOGS
Michelle Jackson

Ida Lee Park

Books and Other Found Things
Allen & Nancy Robinson

For Goodness Sake
Valley Bennett

Leesburg
Farmers Market

North Oatlands Animal Hospital
Dr. Valeria Rickard, DVM

Don's Dahlias
Don & Rhonda Dramstad

Reyes Handyman Service
Pedro Reyes

AV Symington
Aquatic Center

Doggone Natural
Kim Mrozinski

St. John the Apostle
Catholic Church

Singing Stones Animal Wellness
Dr. Carol Lundquist, DVM

Wholistic Paws Veterinary
Dr. Krisi Erwin, DVM

Merlin

I am Merlin "the magician". I know how to flip open the gate to my pen (self-taught of course). I am out in a flash. My job is to keep everyone guessing.

Razz

I am Razz and I love to run and play in the back yard. I taught my brothers how to compete in rally. My job is to patrol the place for cats and squirrels.

Whimze

I am Whimze and I am "the baby" of the family. I will fall down for a belly rub and love treats. Did I tell you I love treats? My job is to make sure there are no crumbs on the carpet.

Our Mom does everything for our Corgi care and convenience. Mom's job is to make sure we all get lots of love, hugs and, of course, treats.

Our Dad also does everything for our Corgi care and convenience (we have them both well trained. Ha!) Dad's job is to drive us to all our fun adventures around town.

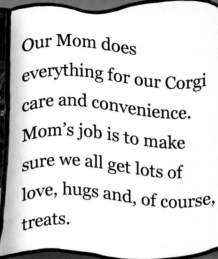

We love to play with Penny. Penny unleashes her creative spirit when she draws our pictures.
Penny's job is to use her amazing talents to bring our true stories to you.